The Boxcar Children® Mysteries

THE DISAPPEARING FRIEND MYSTERY

created by
GERTRUDE CHANDLER WARNER

Illustrated by Charles Tang

ALBERT WHITMAN & Company
Morton Grove, Illinois

Library of Congress Cataloging-in-Publication Data

Warner, Gertrude Chandler, 1890-1979.
The disappearing friend mystery / created by Gertrude Chandler Warner;
illustrated by Charles Tang.
p. cm.—(The Boxcar Children mysteries)
Summary: At the same time that the Alden children's efforts to raise money
for a new hospital are being sabotaged by nasty tricks, they find their attempts
to befriend the new girl, Beth, frustrated by her strange behavior.
ISBN 0-8075-1627-9 (hardcover).
ISBN 0-8075-1628-7 (paperback).
[1.Moneymaking projects—Fiction. 2. Mystery and detective stories.]
I. Tang, Charles, ill. II.Title. III.Series: Warner,
Gertrude Chandler, 1890–Boxcar children mysteries.
PZ7.W244Di 1992   92-32206
[Fic]--dc20   CIP
                                              AC

Cover art by David Cunningham.

Contents

CHAPTER 1

A New Friend

The Alden children, Henry, Jessie, Violet, and Benny, were in the supermarket shopping for groceries. Henry, who was fourteen, was pushing the cart. Twelve-year-old Jessie was holding the grocery list.

The Greenfield supermarket was crowded. Families went up and down the aisles filling their carts. Benny, the youngest of the Aldens, watched the other shoppers and the food they were buying with interest.

"All this shopping is making me awfully hungry," Benny said. He was six. He looked hopefully at his ten-year-old sister, Violet, who was in charge of getting the things off the shelves as Jessie read the list. "Could we get some peanut butter, Violet?"

Violet laughed softly. "Oh, Benny, I'm sure there's plenty of peanut butter at home. Mrs. McGregor always keeps it on hand for you."

"But we *might* need more," said Benny. "Maybe it's on the list."

Jessie, who was very organized, looked at the paper in her hand. "It's not on the list, Benny. But we can get a little more, I think."

"Oh, good," said Benny. He hurried ahead to the peanut butter. He studied all the different jars carefully, then chose one and took it back to the cart.

"It sure is crowded here today," said Henry. "Good thing we're almost done."

"Don't forget the flour, Violet," Jessie

said. She looked down at her list as Henry pushed the cart around to the end of the aisle.

"Oops!" he exclaimed, turning quickly sideways. He had almost run into another shopping cart.

"Wow!" cried Benny. "Look at all that food!"

"I'm sorry," said Henry to the sturdy, brown-haired girl who was pushing the very full cart. She was wearing jeans and a long-sleeved blue shirt. She looked as if she were Jessie's age. Her dark brown, chin-length hair was pulled back with a blue head-band.

The girl smiled, and her blue eyes crinkled. "That's all right," she said. She looked at Benny. "It *is* a lot of food, isn't it? We're new in town, and I'm doing some grocery shopping for my parents."

"Do you have a big family?" asked Benny. "With lots of brothers and sisters? These are my sisters and my brother, and we have a dog named Watch."

"We don't have a dog," said the girl. "But I like them."

"Oh, Benny," said Jessie apologetically. "Hi. My name is Jessie Alden. This is Henry, and Violet. And Benny, of course."

"Hi. I'm glad to meet you. My name is Beth Simon."

"Welcome to Greenfield, Beth," said Violet.

"Thank you very much," said Beth. "I like it here already. I hope we can stay a while — this time."

"Why wouldn't you stay here in Greenfield?" asked Benny.

"My parents are consultants for new companies. We have to move a lot," she said.

"It must be fun seeing lots of new places," said Jessie.

Beth paused. "Well, it is. But it's not always easy to meet people."

The Aldens and Beth had been walking slowly down the aisle as they talked. At the end of the aisle was a community bulletin board. Benny had stopped in front of it and was studying the signs.

"*Help the . . . Help the ho . . .*" he read aloud as Beth and Henry pushed the shopping carts closer.

"Hospital," said Jessie. "The sign says that they're building a new wing on the Greenfield hospital. They're trying to raise money for it."

"How?" asked Benny.

"They're asking people to donate money," explained Jessie.

"Can anybody give money?" asked Benny. "Could we?"

"If we had some to give them, we could," said Henry. He stopped the cart and looked at the other Aldens. "Maybe we could do that."

"What do you mean?" Benny asked.

"We could *earn* money to give to the hospital," Henry said.

"Yes," said Jessie. "We could hold a car wash."

"Or baby-sit," chimed in Violet.

"Or have a bake sale," said Benny, his eyes twinkling at the thought.

Henry grinned at his little brother. "Those all sound like good ideas."

"Well," said Beth. "Why not do them *all*?"

"What do you mean?" asked Henry. "How could we do that?"

Beth turned her cart up the next aisle and Henry did the same with his. They walked slowly, pushing their carts as they talked and shopped.

"Well, where I used to live, my friends and I made money by having a helper service," said Beth. "People could call us for whatever they needed — baby-sitting, car washing, leaf-raking, or dog walking. . . ."

"Or errands or cleaning or whatever," said Jessie excitedly. "What a great idea, Beth."

Beth's cheeks turned pink. "Thank you," she said.

Violet spoke up. "Why don't you work with us, since you thought of it? It would be lots of fun."

Beth hesitated for a minute. Then she said, "I'd love to."

"I'd still rather have a bake sale," said Benny.

"Maybe we still will," said Violet, smiling.

"We need to make posters to advertise," said Jessie. "Beth, could you come over tomorrow? We could all make them together."

Again Beth hesitated. "I . . . think so. Okay!"

"Oh, good," said Benny. "You can meet Watch. And Grandfather. And Mrs. Mc-Gregor — she's our housekeeper. And you can see our boxcar."

The Aldens couldn't help but smile at Beth's puzzled look. They explained how they had lived in a boxcar before they'd come to Greenfield to live with their grandfather Alden. They were orphans, and had run away when they'd heard that Grandfather was a mean person. When he had found them and their boxcar, they'd realized how kind he was and how silly they'd been to run away. They had gone to live with him, and they'd been happy there ever since.

"And Grandfather moved the boxcar so it's behind our house and we can visit it whenever we want," Benny said.

"I can hardly wait to see your boxcar, and to meet Watch, and to make posters," said Beth.

"Where do you live?" asked Henry.

When Beth told him, he said, "Good. That's not far from where we live. You'll be able to get to our house quickly, especially if you have a bicycle."

"I do," said Beth. "Should I bring anything?"

"We have plenty of art supplies," said Violet. "Can you come around ten o'clock?"

"I think so," said Beth.

"Who do we give the money to?" asked Benny suddenly.

"The hospital," said Violet.

"We should find out who's in charge at the hospital," said Jessie.

"We can stop by there after we drop off the groceries," Henry said.

They stopped at the end of the next aisle. Jessie consulted the grocery list. "That's everything," she announced.

They waited while Henry explained to Beth how to get to their house. Then Beth looked at her very full grocery cart. "I'd better hurry. I still have some more shopping to do. I hope the grocery store can deliver all this!"

"If we had our errand service, we could do it!" Henry said, laughing. "But the store delivers."

"Good," said Beth. She waved cheerfully and pushed her cart back up the aisle. "See you tomorrow."

"See you tomorrow," echoed the Aldens.

They paid for their groceries and started to walk home.

"Beth is nice," said Violet.

"And that was a great idea she had," said Henry.

"I think so, too," said Jessie. "I hope Beth has fun doing it with us. For a minute, I didn't think she was going to agree to join us."

"She's probably just a little shy," said Violet, who could understand because she was a little shy herself.

"That's true. And it's a little scary to move to a new place," Jessie said.

"This will be an adventure," said Benny. "Having lots of jobs and making money for the new hospital wing."

The Aldens didn't know it then, but this new project would be not just an adventure, but a *mystery*.

CHAPTER 2

Angry Words

The Greenfield Hospital was a big, old red-brick building near the center of town. The Aldens pedaled up the long driveway that led to the main entrance and parked their bikes outside.

"Where do we go to find out more about the fund-raising for the new hospital wing?" Henry asked the receptionist behind the desk.

"Fund-raising?" The young man raised his eyebrows in surprise.

"Yes," said Jessica. "We would like some more information."

"Oh." The young man pointed down a hall opposite the desk. "Go down that hall all the way to the end to Public Relations. It's the last door on the right."

"Thank you," said Violet.

In the Public Relations Department, the assistant asked them to wait. The Aldens sat down on a long sofa on one side of the office.

Just then, a tall, thin, red-haired woman in a gray suit came into the office.

"Is the director in?" she asked the assistant.

"Yes, but — " the assistant began to answer.

The tall woman didn't stop to listen. She marched angrily across the office, pushed open the door, and went in.

"Wow!" said Henry.

The assistant, a young woman, looked very nervous. She jumped up and followed the tall woman.

Through the door, the Aldens could hear everything that was being said.

"I'm sorry, Mr. Alvarez," said the assistant.

"That's all right, Ms. Grady," a man's voice said.

Then the red-haired woman said firmly, "Mr. Alvarez, Silver City needs a new hospital much more than Greenfield needs a new wing. This is *not* fair! We *won't* stand for it!"

"Doctor, I can understand why you are so upset," said Mr. Alvarez. "But, if you remember, this decision was made by the entire County Board. All the board members agreed that it would be much better to add a new wing to the Greenfield Hospital."

"Not if *I* have anything to do with it!" said the doctor. A moment later Mr. Alvarez's door swung wide open and the red-headed doctor strode out. She didn't even notice the Aldens. She marched out of the office and slammed the door behind her so hard that the pictures on the wall rattled.

"Wow!" said Benny, echoing what Henry had said a moment before.

Ms. Grady, the assistant, came out a moment later. Her face was pale.

"Mr. Alvarez will see you now," she said, sinking down in her chair. She didn't look too happy.

Thanking Ms. Grady, the Aldens went into Mr. Alvarez's office.

Mr. Alvarez, who had brown eyes and black hair with gray streaks in it, looked as upset as his assistant. But he smiled at the children. "Hello," he said. "I'm Mr. Alvarez. What can I do for you?"

"We'd like to know more about the fund-raising drive for the new wing for the Green-field Hospital," said Jessie.

Seeing Mr. Alvarez's slightly puzzled look, Henry explained carefully, "We want to help. We'd like to raise money to contribute."

"That is very generous of you," said Mr. Alvarez. "If only everyone felt the same

way." He shook his head. He walked over to a table that had a model of a building on it. He beckoned the Aldens to join him. "This is a model of what the new wing will look like. It will have the latest in emergency room equipment. We are very proud of it.

"We also are proud that a very wealthy person, who wishes to remain anonymous, has offered to match the amount of money we raise."

"So if you raise a thousand dollars, they'll give you a thousand dollars, too?" said Violet.

"That's right." Mr. Alvarez nodded. "So any money you give will count for twice as much."

"That's great!" Henry said. "But whom do we give the money to?"

"You can give it to me. I'll give you a receipt, and the money will go into the Hospital Building fund at the bank."

"Thank you," said Jessie. "We're going to start earning money tomorrow."

Mr. Alvarez smiled. He didn't seem quite as upset as he had when the Aldens had first come into his office. "Your donation will be greatly appreciated," he said.

The Aldens left the hospital and rode slowly home through the late afternoon shadows.

"I wonder why that red-haired doctor was so angry," said Jessie as they pedaled down the street.

"Maybe she's from Silver City," suggested Violet.

Jessie said thoughtfully, "But you would think a doctor would be glad to have a new wing on a hospital, no matter where it was built."

"Yes," said Henry. "It is very puzzling. But I don't see how she can stop the new wing from being built, especially if it's already been voted on and decided."

"We'll ask Grandfather tonight at dinner," said Henry. "He might know."

Benny had ridden ahead. Now he looked

back over his shoulder. "Let's race home!" he cried. "One, two, three, go!" He took off, pedaling as fast as he could.

"Hey, Benny," shouted Henry, "no fair! You got a head start!" But he and Jessie and Violet began to pedal as fast as they could, too. The four Aldens raced into the driveway of the big old place where they lived. Benny got to the house first.

"I won, I won," he cried gleefully.

"You sure did," said Violet, chuckling. "Come on, let's get ready for dinner."

Laughing, the Aldens went into the house.

CHAPTER 3

At the Ice Cream Parlor

"What have you been doing today?" asked Grandfather as they were finishing dinner that evening.

"We went shopping for Mrs. McGregor," Henry answered. "And we met someone new."

"A new friend?" Grandfather Alden smiled.

"She's coming tomorrow to see our boxcar," Benny said.

"And to meet Watch, Benny, don't forget," Jessie teased. "Her name is Beth Simon, and her family just moved into town, Grandfather. She's going to help us with a project."

"That sounds interesting," said Grandfather.

"We're going to help raise money for a new wing for the hospital," explained Violet. "At the grocery store we saw a sign asking people to donate money."

"An excellent idea." Grandfather nodded approvingly. "The hospital needs a new wing. Having it will help many people."

"But, Grandfather," said Jessie, "we went by the hospital today, to find out more about the fund-raising. We spoke to Mr. Alvarez, who's in charge. While we were there, we heard a doctor arguing with him about the new wing."

"Yes," Henry said. "She was very angry. She said Silver City needed a new hospital more than the Greenfield Hospital needed a new wing."

Grandfather's eyebrows drew together. "Some people did feel that way, when the new wing was first proposed," he said. "But the County Board finally decided that it would be better to have one big hospital all in one place. With two small hospitals, they would always need to buy two of everything. But with one big hospital, more money could be spent on the latest medical equipment."

"That makes sense," said Jessie thoughtfully. "I wonder why that doctor was so angry."

"Anyway, we're going to start a helping service," said Violet. "We will baby-sit, wash cars, run errands, and do whatever else people want done."

"And maybe we'll have a bake sale," said Benny.

Then the Aldens all began to talk at once, telling their grandfather about Beth's idea and the posters they planned to make and all the jobs they could do.

Grandfather laughed. "It all sounds good.

But, meanwhile, why don't we go to the ice cream parlor for dessert? Is that a good idea?"

Benny bounced in his chair. "It's a great idea, Grandfather!"

Soon the Alden family was driving along the quiet streets of Greenfield. Grandfather parked the car and they headed toward the ice cream parlor, with Benny leading the way.

"We can put posters in all these stores," said Henry as they walked down Main Street.

"I'm sure you will have requests for all kinds of jobs," said Grandfather.

In the ice cream parlor, several tables were full. But the Aldens found one near the corner. After a few minutes, the waitress came to take their order.

Henry had a double-scoop cone of chocolate chip mint. Jessie had peach ice cream with whipped cream in a bowl. Violet chose plain blackberry sherbet. She liked it because it was almost the shade of violets, her favorite color. Grandfather had one scoop of vanilla with chocolate syrup. Benny asked for a banana split.

"Can you eat all that?" asked Grandfather.

"I'll try very hard," Benny promised, laughing.

"Okay," said Grandfather. "And I'll help you if you have trouble."

"Okay," said Benny.

Just then, Jessie saw a familiar figure. "Look! There's Beth."

The Aldens turned and saw Beth standing at the counter. Her dark brown hair was pulled back with a red headband and she was wearing a skirt and a red-striped T-shirt.

Jessie jumped up. "I'll go get her and then you can meet her, Grandfather," she said.

Beth had just finished talking to the young woman behind the counter as Jessie came up. "Yes," the woman said. "That's plenty for four people."

"Then that's exactly what I want," said Beth.

"Hi, Beth," said Jessie.

Beth quickly turned around. She looked startled. "Oh!"

"Are you buying ice cream for your family, too? asked Jessie.

"Yes," said Beth.

"While they're getting it ready, come meet our grandfather," Jessie suggested happily.

"But, well, my ice cream will melt," Beth objected.

"You'll be back by the time they have it ready," promised Jessie, leading Beth toward the table where all the Aldens were sitting.

"This is our grandfather, James Henry Alden," said Jessie. "Grandfather, this is Beth Simon."

Grandfather stood up. "Welcome to Greenfield, Beth. Would you like to join us?"

"No. Uh, I mean, no, thank you. Um, I

can't." Beth said quickly. "I have to go. Good-bye."

She hurried back to the counter, although her order wasn't quite ready.

"I'll write out the directions to our house on this napkin," said Violet. "Just so she remembers."

Violet began to scribble down the directions. Jessie waved at Beth, motioning her to come over as she left the counter.

For a moment, Beth hesitated. It didn't look as if she wanted to stop to talk to them again. But then she did.

"I wrote down the directions to our house," said Violet, holding out the napkin. "Just in case you need them when you come over tomorrow."

"Tomorrow?" said Beth.

"At ten o'clock — to make the posters to help raise money for the new hospital wing," said Violet. "You haven't forgotten, have you?"

"No. I didn't forget. Ten o'clock," repeated Beth. She reached eagerly for the instructions and tucked them in the pocket of her skirt. "Thanks. This will be a big help."

"See you tomorrow, Beth," the Aldens called after her as she started toward the door.

Pausing, Beth looked back. Then she nodded uncertainly and hurried out.

The Aldens ate their ice cream slowly and watched the other people in the shop.

"You ate all of yours," Grandfather said as Benny finished the last bite of his banana split.

"This is the best ice cream I ever had," said Benny.

"You always say that, Benny," said Henry.

"It always is," said Benny.

It was time to go home. As they drove toward their house, they talked about seeing Beth again.

"Beth seemed very nervous tonight," Henry said. "I wonder why."

"I think she's just shy," said Violet. "We

should be extra nice to her until she feels more comfortable."

"I think you're right," said Jessie. "And if we get a lot of jobs, Beth will learn her way around Greenfield in no time."

"I guess you're right." Henry said. "It will be fun making posters and working together. That will help Beth feel more at home, too."

Grandfather smiled as he listened to the children.

CHAPTER 4

The Boxcar Helpers

Henry, Jessie, Violet, and Benny had begun to gather their art supplies together the next morning when someone knocked on the front door.

"I'll get it," said Benny. He hurried to the front door with Watch close behind him. When he opened it, Beth was standing on the porching, smiling shyly.

"Hi!" said Benny. He led Beth back through the house. "Here's Beth!" he said.

"Hello," everyone said.

"Hello," said Beth, "May I carry something?"

"Thanks," said Violet, who had been struggling with the blank poster boards. She gave half of them to Beth.

"Come on, then," said Henry.

Beth and the Aldens left the house and went across the backyard toward their boxcar.

"It's really a *real* boxcar!" Beth exclaimed.

"Yes," Jessie said, smiling. "It really is."

"It's wonderful." Beth stopped to study it.

Henry stepped up on the old stump that they used for the front steps and went into the boxcar, followed by Benny, Violet, and Jessie.

Benny leaned out the door of the boxcar. "Come see this inside, Beth!"

So Beth climbed inside and carefully propped the blank poster boards against the wall next to Violet's. She looked around admiringly. There on the shelf was the old knife that the Alden children had used to cut bread and butter, and vegetables, firewood, and string. The big kettle they'd used for cooking was there, and a blue cloth was spread on the table. Beth saw a pitcher and a teapot. Suddenly she heard a loud noise and jumped.

"What is that?" Beth asked.

Henry laughed. "Oh, that's just Benny, ringing the dinner bell."

Beth looked out the door and saw that Benny was ringing an old tin can hung over a branch.

Climbing back into the boxcar, Benny grinned. "I'll show you my cup when we get back to the house," he promised. Benny had a cracked pink cup that he had found when they lived in the boxcar. It was one of his most favorite things in the world, and he still used it.

But now it was time to go to work. Violet had carefully arranged all the art supplies so that they were easy for everyone to reach. The Aldens and Beth sat down at the table.

"First let's decide what we're going to call ourselves," suggested Jessie.

"How about 'The Helpers,' " said Benny.

"Or maybe 'The Boxcar Helpers,' " said Violet.

Everyone liked Violet's idea.

"Now you need to figure out how much you're going to charge for each choice," Beth said.

"And where we're going to put the posters up," Henry added. "And how many we need to make."

"It's a good thing there are a lot of us," said Benny. "That will make deciding easier!"

"It doesn't always," laughed Henry. "What do you think, Beth? Do you have brothers and sisters? Do you always agree on everything?"

"I don't think anyone ever *always* agrees,"

answered Beth. "Not even brothers and sisters."

Violet nodded. "Even if your brothers and sisters are your best friends."

Beth didn't say anything. Then Henry said, "Well, let's start deciding what we'll do then."

The Aldens and Beth talked it over and soon decided what skills they wanted to advertise, and how much to charge for each kind of job. After that it was easy to think of all the places in town they could put up posters.

"We will have to use all of our poster boards, then," said Jessie. "We'd better get started."

But just then, Mrs. McGregor's friendly face appeared in the door of the boxcar.

"How's your project coming along?" she asked.

"We're The Boxcar Helpers," said Benny proudly. "We do everything."

"Just like Charlie the Fix-it Man," said Mrs. McGregor.

"Who's that?" asked Violet.

"You've probably seen his truck around town. It says on the side of it, *No Job Too Big, No Job Too Small, Just Call Charlie*," quoted Mrs. McGregor. "He's a handyman."

"That's a good slogan." Henry laughed. "I wish we'd thought of it! Only we're not fix-it people. We just help out."

"Well, anyway, I've made some chocolate-chip cookies. Would you like some?" she asked.

"Would I!" cried Benny excitedly, jumping up.

"Yes, please," said Beth.

"Yes for all of us," said Jessie.

So they went with Mrs. McGregor back to the kitchen. Benny got his pink cup from the cupboard and sat down at the kitchen table, and everyone joined him. The big, friendly kitchen was filled with the smell of warm cookies.

"Chocolate-chip cookies are my favorite," said Benny as Mrs. McGregor set a plate of delicious-looking cookies on the kitchen table.

"*All* cookies are your favorite," teased Mrs. McGregor. She gave Henry the pitcher of milk, and he poured everyone a tall glassful and filled Benny's pink cup.

"If chocolate chip wasn't my favorite before, it would be now," said Beth. "These cookies are wonderful, Mrs. McGregor."

Mrs. McGregor looked pleased. "Thank you." She paused, then said, "You know, Beth, when you start painting, you might get spots on your clothes."

"Oh!" Beth looked at the Aldens. They were all wearing old clothes. Henry had on jeans and one of his grandfather's patched shirts. Violet was wearing cut-off jeans and a very faded tank top that had once been violet. Jessie had on a white T-shirt that already had paint stains on it and a pair of plain, paint-speckled shorts. Benny was wearing his favorite old overalls, with an old T-shirt, too.

Then Beth looked down at the crisp white shorts and blue-and-white striped T-shirt she was wearing. "You know, I didn't even think of that."

"Why don't I go get one of Mr. Alden's old shirts from my mending basket?" suggested Mrs. McGregor. "I'm sure he won't mind."

"Thank you, Mrs. McGregor. That would be great," said Beth. "And I'll still try to keep it clean."

"I'll be right back," said Mrs. McGregor, walking out of the kitchen. "I know just where they are."

"I have all kinds of ideas for posters," said Violet. She tilted her head to one side, as if she could see all of the ideas lined up in front of her.

"Something with violets on it, I'm sure," Jessie said, teasing her sister with affection.

"Flowers *would* be good on a poster for hospital fund-raising," agreed Violet with a good-natured smile.

"I can't wait to start!" Benny said excitedly.

"Now you can at least wait for Beth, can't you?" Henry said with a twinkle in his eye.

Mrs. McGregor came back into the kitchen and handed Beth one of Mr. Alden's old blue work shirts.

"That is just right!" exclaimed Beth. "Thank you."

"You can go change in my room," said Violet. "It's the first one at the top of the stairs at the end of the hall. You can't miss it."

"I'll be right back," said Beth, running from the room.

The Aldens finished their cookies and milk slowly, trying to make them last.

After several minutes had passed, Violet said, "Maybe Beth got lost. Maybe I should go look for her." She had just pushed her chair back from the kitchen table when Beth came running breathlessly into the kitchen.

"Look. The shirt covers my shorts, so I won't get paint on them, either," said Beth.

"Come on," said Jessie. "Let's get to work on those posters!"

CHAPTER 5

Mean Jokes

Jessie led the way to the boxcar and up the stump step. Then she stopped so quickly that the others almost ran into her.

"Jessie, what is it?" said Henry, sounding puzzled.

"Look!" said Jessie, sounding even more puzzled.

The table where they had left their art supplies was almost completely empty. The only things left were the glasses of water for the watercolors. The paints, pencils, poster boards — even the paintbrushes were gone!

"Did you put away the art supplies before we went for cookies, Jessie?" Henry knew that Jessie always liked to keep things clean and tidy.

But Jessie shook her head. "No," she said.

"Maybe they fell on the floor," said Beth quickly.

"I could understand if *some* of the art supplies fell on the floor," said Henry. "But not all of them at once."

"Besides, they didn't," Violet pointed out.

It was true. Nothing at all was on the floor of the old boxcar.

"Maybe Watch ate them!" cried Benny.

They all looked at Watch, who was standing on the stump with his front paws just inside the door.

"Woof." Hearing his name, Watch barked happily and wagged his tail.

"Watch didn't eat them," said Violet. "He was lying on his old blanket just inside the kitchen door while we had cookies."

"Well, the art supplies are definitely gone," said Henry, who had been walking around the boxcar, looking everywhere for them. "Someone must have come in and taken them."

"Why would anyone want to do that?" asked Beth.

"I don't know." Henry shook his head sadly.

"This is very strange," said Jessie. "But we can't worry about it right now. Let's go get some more supplies so we can get started on our project."

The Aldens and Beth got on their bicycles and pedaled into town to the art store. As they were parking their bikes, Beth said, "Oh, I almost forgot. My mother wanted me to pick something up for her at the drugstore. I'll go next door and do that and meet you in the art store."

"Okay," said Jessie.

The woman who owned the art store was dressed in a black leotard and a big skirt covered with splashes of color just like paint. She smiled cheerfully at the children as they pushed open the door. "Hello! What can I do for you today?" she asked.

"We need some new art supplies," explained Jessie. "We were making posters to help raise money for the new hospital wing. But then someone took all our supplies!"

"That's too bad." The art store owner frowned. But then her smile came back. "Since these posters are to help raise money for the new hospital wing, I'll give you a discount on supplies. That will be my contribution."

"Oh, thank you so very much," said Violet softly.

With the help of the owner, the Aldens had just finished paying for new paints and poster boards when Beth came hurrying in. She was holding a paper bag and seemed a little out of breath.

"Don't worry," said Jessie. "We wouldn't have left without you."

"Are you all finished, then?" Beth looked around nervously.

"Yes," said Benny. "Let's go."

"Oh, Well. I guess . . . yes. Let's go," said Beth. She clutched the bag to her side and went with Benny out of the store. Jessie, Violet, and Henry gathered up the supplies and followed them.

But as they began to put the supplies in their baskets, Benny suddenly exclaimed, "Oh, no!"

"What is it?" asked Jessie.

"My tire is flat!" cried Benny.

"That's strange," said Jessie.

Henry looked more closely at Benny's bike. "This is even stranger — *both* tires are completely flat!"

"But how could *that* happen?" Violet asked.

"This couldn't be an accident," said Henry. "Someone must have let the air out of your tires."

"Really?" said Benny. "Why would anyone do that?"

"Yes, why?" asked Violet.

"Beth," said Jessie. "After you left the drugstore, did you see anybody?"

"W-what do you mean?" asked Beth.

"Anybody near our bikes," Jessie explained.

"Or anybody acting suspicious, as though they might be up to something," suggested Henry.

"No!" said Beth. "No, I didn't. Not at all."

Violet looked at Beth. Beth's face was flushed and she looked almost as if she might cry. "Oh, Beth. Don't worry. We can put more air in the tires," said Violet.

"M-maybe it was someone's idea of a joke," said Beth.

"If it is, it's not a very funny one," said Jessie.

"Can my tires be fixed?" asked Benny anxiously.

"Of course they can, Benny," said Violet.

"We'll go to the bike store and use their pump."

Beth suddenly wheeled her bike away. "I can't go with you," she said.

"But what about the posters?" asked Henry.

"It's getting late. My parents want me to be home soon," Beth said.

"Well, come over tomorrow," suggested Jessie. "We can work on the posters then."

"Uh — okay," said Beth. She quickly got on her bicycle and rode away.

The Aldens walked toward the bike store, wheeling their bicycles. "Why did that upset Beth so much?" wondered Violet.

"Maybe she doesn't like mean jokes," said Henry.

"*I* don't, either," said Benny.

"No one does," said Jessie. "What can Beth think of Greenfield?"

"I wish we had brought Watch," said Benny. "He would have watched my bicycle."

"And I wish Watch had been in the boxcar when our art supplies disappeared. Then they wouldn't have," said Violet with a sigh.

Suddenly, Jessie pointed, "Look! It's Charlie the Fix-it Man's truck. He must be the man Mrs. McGregor was talking about."

Parked on the curb ahead of them was an old white truck, with Charlie's name, phone number, and advertising slogan on it. There was no one in the truck.

"I wonder what's he's fixing," said Violet.

"Do you think we're going to do some of the same kinds of jobs he does?" said Jessie worriedly.

"Maybe," said Henry. "If he were around, we could ask."

But they didn't see anybody near the truck, so they kept on walking toward the bicycle shop, forgetting about Charlie the Fix-it Man.

When they reached the shop, they parked their bikes outside.

"Why don't all of you take Benny's bike inside and pump up the tires," Henry said. "I'll wait here and keep and eye on our bikes, just in case!"

CHAPTER 6

Paint Footprints

The next morning was bright and sunny. The old boxcar seemed almost to shine as the Alden children walked toward it, carrying the new art supplies. Watch barked and pranced happily alongside.

"We'll have plenty of time to make posters today," said Violet as she led the way into the old boxcar. She looked around. It was a comfortable place to be, friendly and full of good memories.

Jessie began to arrange the new supplies neatly on the table.

"I'll fill the old pitcher with water," said Benny. He took the white pitcher off the shelf. Violet had found it in the dump when they lived in the boxcar.

"That's a very good idea, Benny," said Henry.

So Benny went to get water for the watercolors with Watch following friskily at his heels.

"It won't matter that we didn't get to make posters yesterday," said Henry. "We can make twice as many today."

When Benny and Watch got back with the water, Henry, Jessie, and Violet had already settled down around the table.

"Here's a place for you, Benny," said Violet. "I've put a poster board out for you and a pencil so you can draw your design first."

"Will you write the words for me?" Benny asked Violet as he slid into his seat.

"Of course I will," said Violet. "Just tell me what you want to say."

"I'll have to think about that," said Benny.

He paused, then added, "It will probably make me hungry soon."

"Oh, Benny. We just had breakfast." Jessie laughed.

The Aldens got to work. They had made several posters when Beth appeared in the doorway of the boxcar. She was holding Mr. Alden's old shirt, neatly washed and folded. She had on her own old clothes today — cut-off jeans and a faded blue work shirt.

"Hi, Beth," said all the Aldens.

"Hi," said Beth cheerfully.

"I'll take the shirt to Mrs. McGregor," said Benny, jumping up.

"I can do that, Benny," Beth said.

"That's okay," answered Benny. "Mrs. McGregor might have some biscuits left over from breakfast."

Everyone laughed as Benny hurried back to the house.

"Oh, look!" Beth looked at all the posters the children had already made. They were lined up neatly around the room to dry. "These are wonderful." She turned to the

Aldens and smiled. "I'll have to get start-ed!"

Rolling up her sleeves, and grabbing a paintbrush, Beth sat down at the table. Soon she had finished her first poster and had started on her second one.

"You're an excellent artist, Beth," said Henry, admiring the neat drawing of a girl walking a dog. "That looks just like Jessie."

"It's supposed to," Beth said, looking pleased.

"And that's Watch!" exclaimed Jessie, happily.

"Yes, it is!" Beth nodded. Her smile became a huge grin. "This is so much fun. I thought when we moved it would be hard to make new friends. But it hasn't been hard at all. You're all so nice and friendly."

Henry suddenly got up and went to the door. "Benny hasn't come back yet. Do you think he found some biscuits?"

"Probably!" said Jessie. "I could use a break, too."

"I know!" said Violet excitedly. "Let's each take a poster in and show it to Grandfather."

"We can have a poster show!" said Jessie. "It will be hard to pick out the best ones, though."

"I know which poster I'm choosing," said Jessie, and she carefully picked up the one Beth had made of Jessie walking Watch, to advertise dog walking.

So Beth and Henry and Violet each chose a poster and went up to the house to show their work to Grandfather Alden.

"Oh — maybe we should bring one of Benny's, too," Beth suggested. "I'll run back and get one."

"Okay," said Jessie as Beth headed back to the boxcar.

Grandfather Alden was in his study with a tall dark-haired man. When Grandfather looked up and saw the children standing at the door, he motioned for them to come in. "I have some people here you'll be glad to see," Grandfather said to his guest.

The man turned and smiled. "Your grandchildren!" he said.

"Dr. Moore," said Henry. He shook hands with Dr. Moore. Then Jessie and Violet did, too.

Dr. Moore had given Henry work when the Aldens were living in their boxcar, before Grandfather found them. It was Dr. Moore who had figured out the mystery of Grandfather's missing grandchildren. And it was Dr. Moore who had helped bring Grandfather Alden and the Alden children together at last.

"What do you have here?" asked Dr. Moore, noticing the colorfully painted poster boards.

"We've started a job service called The Boxcar Helpers. We want to help raise money for the new wing at the Greenfield Hospital," explained Jessie.

"A wonderful idea," said Dr. Moore. He looked around. "But where is Benny?"

"Here I am," said Benny. "I was in the kitchen with Mrs. McGregor."

"We've brought some of our posters to show off to Grandfather," Jessie told Dr. Moore.

"I brought one of yours, too, Benny. Here," Beth said, coming into the study with another poster.

The Aldens introduced Beth to Dr. Moore. Then Benny took his poster and held it up proudly.

"It's excellent, Benny," said Grandfather. "All of them are." He paused and looked more closely at the one that Jessie was holding. "Jessie, that looks like you and Watch."

"It is. Beth drew it," Jessie said.

"Very good, Beth." Grandfather nodded approvingly, his eyes twinkling. "I think with posters like these, you will have plenty of people calling with jobs."

"Do you want a new wing built at the Greenfield Hospital, Dr. Moore?" asked Violet.

Dr. Moore looked surprised. "Of course I do, Violet. Why?"

Violet and the others told Dr. Moore about the conversation they'd overheard at the hospital between Mr. Alvarez and the angry doctor.

Dr. Moore looked thoughtful. "Yes, it is true," he said. "Being from Silver City myself, I know some of my neighbors were very upset when the board decided not to build a new hospital there. But I thought everyone had accepted the idea by now. I didn't realize there were still problems."

He looked at the Aldens and Beth. "But don't let that stop you. I will certainly recommend you for any jobs I hear about. I know you're good workers."

"And we'll make lots of money," crowed Benny. "Let's go make lots more posters. Soon we will have enough."

As the Aldens walked back to the boxcar with Beth, they explained who Dr. Moore was. Jessie told Beth how Violet had gotten sick while they were all living in the boxcar, and how Dr. Moore had taken her to his house and made her well again.

Suddenly Benny shouted "Look!" An odd sight met their eyes. On the stump outside the boxcar were footprints — brightly colored paint footprints.

The children looked into the boxcar, where they saw more footprints. "Oh, no!" Jessie cried. The posters were no longer lined up neatly against the wall to dry. They were scattered all over the floor. Water had been poured on some of them, so the paint had run. Some of the posters had paint smeared across them in big, angry slashes. Not a single poster had been left untouched.

"Our posters!" gasped Violet.

"They're ruined," said Henry.

"Who would *do* something like this?" Jessie looked angrily around the boxcar, as if she could catch whoever had done it.

"Maybe it was the wind?" whispered Beth.

"No." Henry shook his head.

"Maybe it was Watch?" Beth offered.

"Watch would never do something like this." Imitating his brother, Benny shook his head vigorously.

Jessie said, "This wasn't an accident. Look at these footprints smeared all around. Someone had to take the paint over to the posters to mess them all up like that."

Beth cleared her throat. "At least we had the best posters inside with us, so they weren't ruined."

The angry look began to leave Jessie's face. "That's true, Beth. Let's clean this up and get back to work."

"Yes. We can always make more posters," agreed Henry. "You know, it's almost as if someone doesn't want us to get started raising money for the new hospital wing."

"But why?" asked Violet. "I don't understand."

"I don't understand it either," said Henry, sounding puzzled.

Luckily, there was plenty of poster board and paint. Everyone got back to work. At last the posters were finished and dry. The children decided to take them into town and put them up before anything else happened.

Every storekeeper quickly agreed to let the

children put up their posters. But when they got to the flower shop, the children had a problem.

As the children walked in the door, a tall woman was turning away from the counter, holding an armful of roses.

"It's her," whispered Jessie. "It's that doctor from the hospital."

The doctor was smiling and smelling her roses. Then she saw the posters.

She stopped. "*The Boxcar Helpers. Let us help you — and help the hospital,*" she read aloud. "What is this?"

"We want to help raise money for the new wing of the Greenfield Hospital," said Henry carefully. "So we've started a helper service."

The doctor frowned. "A helper service," she repeated, as if she couldn't believe what she was hearing.

"Yes," said Violet bravely. "All the money we earn doing odd jobs and errands will go to the hospital for the new wing that will be built."

"Well *I* don't approve," said the doctor. "We don't need a new wing — Silver City needs a new hospital. This is ridiculous."

The doctor's eyes narrowed angrily. She pushed past the children and out the door.

The florist, who had been listening, shook his head.

"Oh, dear," said Jessie. "Does this mean you won't let us put up a poster?"

"Well-ll," said the florist. "She's a good customer. I'd hate to lose her." He paused.

"Please?" said Benny.

"Well," said the florist again, "I guess that new wing is going to be good for business. People often send flowers to patients in the hospital. Okay, you can put your poster up in the front window in the corner."

"Thank you!" said Henry.

Soon they had posters all over town, from the supermarket to the bicycle shop.

Just as they were putting their last poster in the window of the ice cream shop, an older woman passed by and stopped to read it.

"How lovely," she said. She looked at Beth. "That is a very good project, Heather. Your family must be proud. Well, I'll have to remember to call you if I need help with anything."

As the woman left, Henry frowned. "Heather?" he said.

Beth shrugged. "When you're new in town, people get your name mixed up sometimes. It happens to me every time we move." She didn't seem too interested. She put the last piece of tape on the poster and stepped back. "There."

"Now all we have to do is wait for people to call," said Henry.

"I think people will," said Benny. "Lots of people. We'll be very busy!"

"I guess," said Henry. "We should probably have just a *little* ice cream — while we still have some free time!"

"Hooray!" said Benny, leading the way to the ice cream counter.

CHAPTER 7

Beth's Disappearing Trick

The phone rang as Jessie, Violet, Benny, Henry, and Grandfather Alden were finishing breakfast the next morning. A minute later, Mrs. McGregor came into the dining room. She was smiling. "I have a call for The Boxcar Helpers," she said.

"It's our first job," said Jessie excitedly. "Oh, Grandfather, may one of us be excused to see who it is?"

Grandfather laughed. "The early bird gets the worm," he said. "Go on, Jessie."

Jessie slipped quickly away from the table.

Everyone else began to help Mrs. McGregor clear away the dishes. They had just finished when Jessie came back.

"What is it, Jessie?" cried Benny.

"That was a lawyer, Ms. Singh, who is going away on a business trip for two days," Jessie told them. "She wants us to come feed her cats this week while she's gone. She lives over on Garden Street, and she's going to leave the key under the mat by the back door."

"That'll be fun," said Violet. "Only we had better not take Watch!"

The phone rang again. "I'll get it," said Henry.

"Sounds like you're off the a good start," said Grandfather. "I'll leave you to conduct business."

"Let's go see what job this is," said Benny. He and Violet and Jessie joined Henry. Henry hung up the phone and wrote something down carefully.

"Well?" asked Jessie.

"Mr. Hudson, on Hickory Lane, wants his grass cut. I told him I was an expert grass cutter!" Henry laughed. "So while you're feeding cats, I will cut the grass."

The phone rang again, and then again. Soon they had more than enough jobs for the day, and they began to schedule them for the next day and the next.

"We have to tell Beth," said Violet when the phone finally stopped ringing. Quickly she dialed Beth's number. "Hello, Beth?" she said eagerly. Then she frowned. "Oh. Thank you."

A moment later she said again, "Hello, Beth? Is that you? This is Violet Alden speaking."

The others listened as Violet told Beth all about the jobs. "So we'll be busy all day," Violet said. "Are you going to come with us? . . . Oh. That's too bad. Okay, we'll see you tomorrow. Good luck!"

Violet hung up the phone. "Poor Beth. She has to go to the dentist in Silver City today and can't help us."

"Too bad," said Jessie sympathetically. "But we'd better get started."

The Aldens made a list of all the jobs they had to do that day, then went and got their bicycles and pedaled into town to get started. They had just come out of the post office, where they had taken a package to be mailed for someone, when they saw a familiar figure riding her bicycle down the street ahead of them.

"Look!" Violet was startled. "Isn't that Beth?"

Henry raised his hand to shade his eyes. "It sure looks like her. Beth! Hey, Beth!"

The figure didn't turn around.

"Beth!" shouted Benny at the top of his lungs.

This time, Beth turned around. So did several other people on the street.

But Beth didn't stop. She didn't even wave. Instead, she turned around again and pedaled her bicycle even faster.

Surprised, the Alden children watched the figure until she disappeared around a corner.

Henry looked puzzled. "That's strange. Wasn't Beth going to the dentist?"

"That's what she told me," Violet answered.

"Do you think she was lying?" asked Jessie.

"I can't believe she would," said Violet.

"Maybe Beth doesn't like us anymore," suggested Benny.

"No, Benny," said Henry. "That couldn't be it."

"Why didn't she at least stop and say hello?" Jessie wondered.

But they forgot all about Beth as they came around the next corner. One of the posters they had put up on the bulletin board outside the deli had been torn down. It had been ripped apart and trampled.

"I don't believe this," said Henry, stopping his bike.

Jessie looked mad. "Here," she said shortly. "Watch my bike. I'm going in to ask the people in the deli if they saw anything."

But when she came back out a few minutes later, she didn't have any clue to give them.

"I think Henry's right. Somebody really doesn't want us to raise money," said Violet.

"Yes. It's a good thing most of our posters are *inside* the windows of the stores. At least they probably won't get ripped down," said Jessie.

"Maybe it's that doctor," said Benny.

Henry frowned. "Maybe," he agreed slowly. "But it's a funny way for a doctor to act."

Just then Jessie noticed a truck parked on the side of the street. It was the truck that belonged to Charlie the Fix-it Man. As they turned the corner, they saw a small man with a white cap on his head cutting the grass in the backyard of the house. The cap said CHARLIE on the bill.

"So we do work on some of the same jobs," said Henry.

"Could Charlie be the one who tore down

our sign?" asked Violet. "Maybe he doesn't want us taking his business."

"Maybe," said Jessie. She looked at her watch. "We'd better get going. The day's nearly half over and we have a lot of work to do."

The next day, they got two new jobs in addition to the ones scheduled from the day before. One of the jobs was in Beth's neighborhood.

This time, Jessie called her. "Guess what, Beth?" she asked. "The Millers have asked us to come dig their vegetable garden. They live in your neighborhood. So we can come pick you up at your house."

"No!" said Beth so forcefully that Jessie had to hold the phone a little away from her ear. "No," Beth repeated, more quietly, but just as firmly. "It's . . . well, the house is such a mess . . . we haven't finished un-packing. My parents would kill me if I in-vited anyone over."

"Oh. Well," said Jessie slowly, a bit taken

aback by Beth's strong response. "We'll just have to meet you there then." She gave Beth directions to the Millers' house and they agreed to meet in half an hour.

"Did Beth say anything about seeing us yesterday?" asked Henry as the Aldens headed for the Millers' house.

"No," answered Jessie thoughtfully. "Something very strange is going on."

Beth was waiting out front when they got to the Millers'. She waved cheerfully as they pedaled up. "What a great day for gardening," she said.

"I'm glad you could come today," said Violet softly, falling into step by Beth as they walked up to the front door of the house. "How was the dentist?"

Beth made a face. "Oh — the dentist. I don't like going. But at least I didn't have any cavities."

"That's good," said Violet.

"Did you have a lot of jobs yesterday?" Beth asked Violet.

"Lots!" said Violet. "We had to go all over

town, too." She paused, wondering if Beth would mention seeing them.

But Beth just flung out her arms and said, "Great. Soon we'll have enough money to pay for the whole new hospital wing!"

Henry grinned. "Or at least one of the rooms!" he said as he rang the Millers' doorbell.

Mr. Miller was an older man, with a round face and little mustache. He was wearing baggy pants held up by red suspenders, with a red striped shirt to match. He kept his thumbs hooked in the suspenders as he showed the children what he wanted them to do.

He unhooked one of the thumbs to raise his hand and give the children a little wave as he went back into the house.

The Millers had marked off a large square piece of level ground in a sunny area of their backyard for the garden. There were shovels, hoes, and pitchforks for breaking up the ground. Benny collected all the rocks and lined the edge of the garden with them. They pulled up clumps of weeds and took out sticks. Then they made long raised rows of dirt, which would be easy to plant in. Between the rows of mounded dirt, they carefully marked paths. With everyone working together, the Aldens and Beth soon had the garden ready for planting.

As they were working, a truck drove slowly by and then stopped. A wiry little man in faded blue overalls and a blue work shirt leaned out of the window on the driver's side. He pushed the bill of his cap back and squinted over the fence.

It was Charlie, the Fix-it man.

"You kids know what you're doing?" asked Charlie.

"Yes, thank you," said Beth.

"Gardening can be hard work — especially if you aren't used to it," he commented. "Of course I do a lot of it."

"With all of us working together, it goes pretty quickly," Henry said.

"I guess so." Charlie jerked his head to-

ward the house. "I usually do the gardening for the Millers," he said. "Or I used to."

"Oh!" said Violet. No one else could think of anything to say.

"Yep," said Charlie, looking off into the distance. "See you later." He leaned back in the window, put the truck in gear, and drove away.

"Do you think we really are taking work away from Charlie?" asked Jessie.

"I don't know," said Henry, wiping his forehead. It was a very hot day.

"If the Millers usually have Charlie do their gardening, I wonder why they hired us," Violet said.

"Maybe Charlie did something they didn't like," Henry suggested.

Just then Mr. Miller came out onto the back porch and invited the Aldens and Beth in for lemonade.

"Yes, please!" said Benny quickly.

"That would be great," said Henry, propping his shovel against a tree. "We only have a little more to do."

But Beth shook her head regretfully. "I have to go. I promised I'd help out at home today, too."

"You kids are doing a great job," said Mr. Miller.

Beth smiled. "Thank you," she said. "See you tomorrow," she told the Aldens. She went around the side of the house toward her bicycle and everyone else went inside for glasses of cold lemonade. It was delicious. Benny had two glasses.

"Whew," said Henry as they went back outside. "That's hot, thirsty work."

Violet nodded. "I like gardening, but I'm glad we're almost through. . . ."

Her voice trailed off in horror as she looked past Henry at the garden they had so carefully dug.

All the neat rows had been kicked and shoveled every which way. Rocks and sticks and weeds were scattered all over the garden plot. And the soft, crumbly dirt had been stomped down hard.

"Oh, no!" cried Jessie.

"My rocks!" wailed Benny.

They all ran forward to look more closely.

"This is awful," said Violet. "We'll have to do it all over again."

Benny trudged out into the garden and began to pick up rocks.

"Wait a minute, Benny," said Henry. "Maybe we can find some clue to who did this. Like footprints."

But it was impossible to pick out individual footprints because there were so many and the dirt was so scuffed up.

Sadly, the Aldens went back to work. As they worked, they talked about who could have done such an awful thing.

"Why doesn't someone want us to earn money for the hospital?" wondered Henry.

"Maybe it was that doctor," Violet said. "She was very angry about the hospital wing — both times we saw her."

"Did she follow us here?" Benny asked.

"I guess she might have. Or maybe it was Charlie. He may be angry that we're taking some of the jobs he used to do — like this

garden. And he definitely knew we were
here."

"He was just down the street the day we
saw the torn poster," Violet pointed out.

"And he was in town when the air was
being let out of my tires," Benny added.

The children kept working. When they
were almost done Jessie said, "You know
. . . there's another person it could be. Have
you thought about all the strange things that
have happened? They all have something in
common."

"What do you mean?" Violet asked.

"Every time something happened, Beth
had suddenly left — or *disappeared*," Jessie
said. "We were in our kitchen having cookies
and milk when the supplies were taken,
remember?"

Violet said slowly, "Beth was in my room
putting on one of Grandfather's old blue
work shirts."

Nodding, Jessie said, "Right. But she was
gone for a *long* time. Then, when we went
to buy new art supplies . . ."

"Beth said she had to go next door and do some errands. When we came out, someone had let the air out of Benny's bicycle tires," Henry finished.

"And whoever ruined the garden did it while we were inside having lemonade," said Jessie. "And Beth left just before we went inside. Or *said* she was leaving."

"It can't be Beth," cried Violet. "I just *know* Beth wouldn't do anything like this."

"I don't want to believe it either, Violet," said Jessie. "But the clues all seem to point to her."

"It could have been anybody," argued Violet. "It's just a coincidence that makes it look like Beth was the one. Besides, she's new in town. Why wouldn't she want us to help with the hospital?"

"That's true," said Henry doubtfully. "But still . . ."

"Beth's the one who *thought* of the helper service, too," Violet pointed out.

"It doesn't make sense," said Jessie. "But

it is *possible* Beth did all these awful things."

"Well," said Violet stubbornly. "I'm not going to believe it."

The Aldens finished the garden in silence, and went home with heavy hearts.

CHAPTER 8

What's Wrong with Beth?

That evening The Boxcar Helpers got a late night phone call. Jessie answered the phone. "Hello?"

"This is Gail Jackson. I'm sorry to call you so late," a woman's pleasant voice sounded on the phone. "But it's something of an emergency, and I saw your signs for the helper service."

"We'll help you if we can," said Jessie.

"Oh, I hope you can. I need a baby-sitter for Shirley. She's three. I have a meeting I *must* attend, and her regular baby-sitter canceled."

"I think we can help," said Jessie. "But let me call you back."

She carefully wrote down the time and place of the baby-sitting job, then hung up the phone and turned around to talk to the others.

"Mrs. Jackson, over on Walnut Street, needs us to baby-sit for her daughter Shirley tomorrow afternoon from one until four-thirty," she told them.

"Uh-oh," said Henry. "I'm weeding Mrs. Paul's flowerbeds tomorrow afternoon."

"And I'm walking the Peterson's Great Dane," said Jessie.

"I don't think I could baby-sit for a three-year-old by myself," said Violet.

They all looked at Benny. "I'm too young," said Benny. "Aren't I?"

"I'm afraid so, Benny," said Henry.

"Beth and I could do it together," suggested Violet.

"I don't know if we should ask her, Violet. She's been acting awfully strange lately," said Jessie.

"I don't think so," said Violet stubbornly.

"Well." Henry looked thoughtful. "If the two of you were together, what could go wrong?"

"That's true," agreed Jessie.

"Good," said Violet. "Then I'll call Beth and ask her."

Violet did just that, and Beth sounded surprised and pleased. "I'll be there," she assured Violet.

Mrs. Jackson was also pleased when Jessie called her back. "I am so glad," she told Jessie. "Your helper service is a lifesaver!"

The next day, Violet rode her bike over to the Jacksons'. The Jacksons lived on a quiet, shady street near the Aldens. The white house had cheerful blue shutters on the windows, and a big old apple tree out front. Squirrels were running around as Violet pedaled up the driveway.

Violet propped her bicycle against the garage and turned, laughing, to watch the squirrels scampering about. Just then, Beth came riding up the driveway. She skidded to a halt and sent the squirrels scurrying away in fright.

Violet was a little surprised, too.

Beth put her bicycle beside Violet's then walked with Violet up to the front door.

"Right on time," said a firm voice as the front door opened.

"Hello," said Violet softly. "I'm Violet Alden, and . . . oh!"

The woman in the door was tall and thin, and she had bright red hair. She was the angry doctor from the Greenfield Hospital!

"Hello," said the woman. "I'm Dr. Jackson."

"I'm Beth Simon," said Beth.

Violet didn't know quite what to say.

As if she could understand how surprised Violet was, Dr. Jackson said, "Come on in. I had to have a baby-sitter, and I didn't know whom to call. Then I remembered seeing your sign in the flower shop. And, for that matter, seeing the rest of your signs all over Greenfield."

"Oh," said Violet.

"Your service is a good one," said Dr. Jackson. "I don't agree that a new hospital wing is the best idea, but it is better than nothing." She paused and looked thoughtful. "And I admire people, especially young people, who are willing to work for something they believe in. So I decided to call you." Dr. Jackson didn't smile, but she didn't look so stern now.

"Th-thank you," said Violet, still very surprised.

"This is Shirley," said Dr. Jackson. A little girl in neat blue denim overalls, with her hair in two fat pigtails, came up to Dr. Jackson and grabbed her hand.

Violet smiled. "Hello, Shirley."

Shirley looked at Violet thoughtfully. "I'm three," she announced.

Dr. Jackson smiled. "Shirley just had a birthday," she explained. "Shirley, this is Beth and this is . . . ?"

"Violet Alden," said Violet.

"Violet," repeated Dr. Jackson. "They will be staying with you until I come back in a little while. Remember, I told you about that?"

Shirley nodded solemnly.

"Good," said Dr. Jackson. "Now, Beth and Violet, here is a phone number where I can be reached if anything comes up. There's a snack for Shirley when she gets hungry this afternoon in the kitchen — banana pudding and milk. There are other things, too, if *you* get hungry, so please make yourselves at home. I'll be back by four-thirty."

Dr. Jackson kissed Shirley good-bye and hurried out the door.

Violet took Shirley's hand. "You know, I have a brother a little bit older than you. His name is Benny."

Shirley looked at Violet and at Beth. Then she let go of Violet's hand and sat down on the floor and began to cry.

"Mammaaa," howled Shirley.

"Oh, Shirley. Don't cry. Your mother will be back in just a little while."

"Mammmaa," cried Shirley louder.

"Shhh," said Violet soothingly.

"Good grief," said Beth.

Violet took Shirley's hand and pulled her to her feet. "You take her other hand, Beth," she said.

"Why?" asked Beth.

"We'll take her outside in the backyard. If we can get her to play, she'll forget about her mother and stop crying."

In the backyard was a big sandbox full of toys. "Here," said Violet. "We'll build sand castles. Would you like to build sand castles, Shirley?"

Shirley kept crying.

"Good grief, stop it!" snapped Beth, snatching her hand free from Shirley's.

Violet looked at Beth in surprise.

"What a brat," said Beth.

"She's just scared because her mother's gone and we're strangers. If you try to understand, it's not so hard," Violet said.

Beth folded her arms and sat down on the edge of the sandbox. "Well . . . *do* something."

Beth is acting so strangely, thought Violet. Gently she led Shirley into the sandbox. She sat down by her and began to pour sand into the different colored containers.

Watching Violet, Shirley gradually began to stop crying. Then she was only sniffling. Suddenly, she reached out for a container.

"Mine," she said, turning the container upside down to make a square sand tower.

"Good, Shirley," said Violet.

As they played in the sandbox, Violet told Beth about Dr. Jackson and the conversation the Aldens had overheard at the hospital. "We wondered if Dr. Jackson might be the one who didn't want us to raise money for the hospital," said Violet. "But it doesn't look that way, does it? I don't think she played all those terrible tricks on us, do you?"

Beth, who had been sitting on the edge of the sandbox watching, folded her arms. "You never know," she said.

"Well, I don't think it is Dr. Jackson," said Violet. "Are you hungry, Shirley? I think it's time for your snack."

The two girls took Shirley inside for her snack and sat with her. While she ate her banana pudding, Beth and Violet had milk.

"Can you say banana pudding?" Violet asked Shirley.

"Nannaning," said Shirley.

Violet smiled, then looked up. Beth was staring at her.

"Is something wrong?" asked Violet.

Beth jumped. "Wrong? No. Of course not."

But Violet couldn't help but notice how

uncomfortable Beth seemed. She wasn't acting like herself at all.

Maybe her brothers and sister had been
right about Beth, thought Violet. But she
didn't want to believe it.

Violet was relieved when Dr. Jackson
came back, and it was time to go home. Beth
said a quick good-bye to Violet and dashed
off on her bicycle.

That night after dinner, Violet told everyone about the baby-sitting job and Dr.
Jackson.

"Dr. Jackson?" asked Grandfather. "I
know Dr. Jackson. She speaks her mind.
But she is a good doctor, and a good
person."

"We wondered if she would not like us
raising money for the new wing, since she
was against building it," said Jessie. "But it
doesn't look that way now."

"No," said Grandfather. He got up from
the dinner table. "I'll be in my study for a
little while."

After Grandfather left, Jessie said thought-fully, "Still, something strange is going on. Maybe it *is* Beth. You did say she was acting nervous, Violet."

"Maybe we shouldn't be friends with Beth," said Benny.

"That's not fair," protested Violet angrily. "You can't just *stop* being friends with some-one. You have to at least give her a chance."

Henry nodded. "You're right, Violet. Besides, the person who's doing all these mean things could be Charlie the Fix-it Man."

"Well," said Jessie, "I hope we solve this mystery soon. But how are we going to do that?"

No one had an answer.

CHAPTER 9

Two Cats and a Key

"Today we meet Ms. Singh's cats," announced Violet. "I can hardly wait."

Henry, Violet, Jessie, and Beth were waiting for Benny on the front steps of the big old white house.

Just then, Benny came hurrying out of the door. "Here I am!" he announced cheerfully.

"We're going to feed Ms. Singh's cats, Benny," said Jessie.

"Oh, good," said Benny, getting on his

bicycle. "I like cats. Watch does, too. Don't you, Watch?"

Watch barked and began to trot happily alongside Benny's bicycle as they headed for Garden Street.

It wasn't very far away, a pleasant street that lived up to its name.

"Ms. Singh's house has an apple tree in the front yard," said Henry. "She said it's the only one on the street."

"Apples!" exclaimed Benny. "I love apples." Suddenly he pointed. "There it is."

The five children left their bicycles under the apple tree and went around to the back door.

"Let's see," said Jessie. "The key should be under this doormat." She raised the edge of the mat. But there was no key.

"Maybe if you lift up the whole mat," suggested Beth.

Jessie picked up the mat. There was a clean space, slightly paler than the rest of the step, where the mat had been. But there was no key.

"That's funny," said Violet. "Are you sure Ms. Singh said the key would be under the mat?"

"Yes." Jessie frowned. "Maybe I misunderstood her. Maybe it was the *front* door mat."

The Aldens and Beth went around to the front door of the house. But when Jessie lifted the front doormat, no key was under it.

"Maybe Ms. Singh left the key somewhere else, like in the mailbox," suggested Beth.

"I hope so," said Violet, looking worried. "What if we can't find the key? We won't be able to feed the cats."

"Oh, no," cried Benny. "They'll starve."

Henry, who was the tallest, stood on his toes and looked into the mailbox. He reached his hand inside and felt the bottom of the box. "No," Henry reported. "No key here."

"Oh dear," said Violet. "Do you think she forgot?"

"Maybe the key slid out from under the mat somehow," Henry said. "Benny, why don't you and Violet come with me and we'll check around the back door."

"Good idea," said Jessie. "Beth and I will look here in front."

Jessie and Beth searched all around the front door, from the top of the door sill to the flowerbeds on either side, but they found no key.

"It's not here," said Jessie.

"Maybe Henry and Violet and Benny found it," said Beth. "Let's go around to the back door and see."

But the key was nowhere around the back door, either.

"Watch looked, too," Benny announced. "He sniffed and sniffed, but he didn't find a key. So maybe she did forget."

"That's hard to believe," said Violet.

"How are we going to feed the cats?" asked Benny.

Henry said, "If Ms. Singh left a window unlocked, we could open it and go inside that way."

"I don't like having to do something like

that," said Jessie. "But I guess it *is* an emergency."

"Yes, we can't let the cats starve," said Violet.

The children checked the windows on the ground floor, but Ms. Singh had locked them all tightly before leaving. Benny, peering through the kitchen window, said, "I can see one of the cats now! It's big and white, with one black spot right over her eye."

The cat saw Benny, too. She leaped up on the windowsill and meowed. Watch, sitting on the grass, barked. The cat flattened her ears and jumped away from the window.

"You scared her, Watch," scolded Benny.

Just then Jessie called, "Look! There's the basement door! Maybe we can get in that way."

The Aldens and Beth hurried to the back corner of the house and down the narrow stairs to the basement door. It was a little, low door and the basement inside was very dark.

"Ooh," said Benny. "This is scary."

Watch growled softly.

"Oh, no. You can't come with us, Watch. You would chase the cats!" said Jessie scoldingly.

Benny had an idea. "I'll take Watch outside and then meet you at the back door. You can let me in there."

"Good idea, Benny," said Violet.

Relieved, Benny hurried out of the dark basement.

The others made their way carefully across the basement. Then Henry and Jessie went up the creaking basement stairs.

Cautiously, Henry tested the door at the top of the stairs. It was open!

"Thank goodness," said Violet, following them up the stairs with Beth beside her. "Now we can feed the cats!"

The basement door opened into a short hall that led into the kitchen. Beth went to the back door and let Benny in.

"Look, here's a note from Ms. Singh," said Violet. She picked it up from the kitchen table and read aloud, *"Dear Boxcar Helpers, welcome, and thank you for feeding my cats, Spot and Rover.*"

"So she didn't forget we were coming," said Henry.

Violet nodded and kept reading: "*The wet food is on the counter. They each get a small can of wet food, a fresh bowl of water, and please fill the big green bowl with dry food. The dry food is in the bucket with the lid by the refrigerator. Just leave the key under the back doormat where you found it when you are finished. Thank you.*"

Jessie said, "She doesn't sound like she forgot to leave the key."

"It's a mystery," agreed Henry. "But we will solve it!"

Just then, the children heard a clock chime in the living room.

"Uh-oh," exclaimed Beth.

"What is it?" asked Jessie.

"I should be going. My parents wanted me to be home early for lunch today."

"It *is* almost lunchtime," said Henry. "It took us so long to get inside, the morning is almost gone."

"Well, I'll see you later," said Beth.

"I'll walk you to your bicycle," Jessie said.

When Jessie came back in the kitchen she was holding something and looking very puzzled.

"What is it, Jessie?" asked Henry.

"Look." Jessie held out her hand. In the palm was a silver key.

"The house key?" asked Violet.

Jessie nodded. "It fits the door."

"Where did you find it?" asked Benny.

"By the flowerpot at the foot of the back door steps."

"We looked there!" said Benny. "We looked everywhere!"

"I suppose we could have overlooked it," said Henry slowly. "But it doesn't seem likely."

Jessie shook her head. "I don't think we did, either."

"Then how did the key get there?" asked Violet.

Henry handed the key back to Jessie. "I'm

surprised Beth didn't see it on her way out," he said.

"Well," said Violet. "She was in a hurry."

Jessie put the key in her pocket. "Anyway, we'll just keep this key so we can get in tomorrow, and *then* after we feed Spot and Rover tomorrow, we'll put it under the mat."

"Good thinking," said Henry.

"Like Beth said, this has been an adventure," said Jessie.

"I guess so!" said Violet. "Let's hope we don't have any more!"

CHAPTER 10

An Unexpected Customer

Soon a morning came, when the Aldens didn't have any jobs scheduled.

"I know," said Benny. "Let's have a bake sale!"

"Oh, Benny. First we'd have to bake something. It would take too much time," said Henry.

"But we could have a car wash," Jessie suggested. "All you need is soap and water and sponges. We have all those things."

The Aldens all agreed that Jessie's idea was a good one.

"We'll need some soft cloths to dry the cars with after we wash and rinse them," said Henry.

Mrs. McGregor probably has some she could give up," said Violet. "I'll get them from her and call Beth."

So while Violet went to call Beth and get soft cloths from Mrs. McGregor, the others began to gather together all the other things they would need for the car wash. They decided to have it out in front of the house.

"Beth is going to bring an extra piece of poster board," announced Violet as she helped fill the buckets with soap and water. "Then we can make a big sign to put out front."

Beth arrived just as they finished bringing the buckets of soapy water to the edge of the front yard.

"I'll get the hose," said Benny.

Violet and Beth went into the house and

got a marker. Beth wrote CAR WASH $1.00 in big letters and they tied the poster to a tree near the intersection of the road.

"Wait a minute," said Beth. She took the marker and drew an arrow, pointing in the direction of the Aldens' house.

"Good idea," said Violet.

They went back to wait for customers. At first things were slow. Then a lady in a big, blue car drove up. The children went quickly to work with the soapy water and sponges.

"I'll turn on the hose," said Benny when it was time to rinse off the soap. He hurried back to the house. A minute later, before anyone had a chance to pick up the hose, a big jet of water squirted out. The hose squirmed around on the ground like a giant snake, spraying everyone, even Watch, who barked excitedly and ran away from the water.

Jessie and Henry managed to grab the hose.

"Oh, no!" said Benny, running back. "I didn't mean to do that."

"It's okay, Benny." Beth laughed. "We'll dry off quickly."

They finished washing the blue car, and the woman gave them their money. "You did a good job," she said.

They had just had time to dry off in the warm sun when another car drove up, and right behind it, another. They had two cars to wash at once! Beth and the Aldens set to work.

It was a very busy morning. They washed a little red car that belonged to a young woman who kept telling them she was in a hurry. They washed a very old car that belonged to veterinarian who had two dogs in the car with him. The dogs in the car and Watch barked at one another and wagged their tails happily. They even washed one boy's bicycle for twenty-five cents. Then business slowed down again.

"Whew," said Violet. "Washing cars is hard work."

"I know," said Benny, "let's wash Grandfather's car as a surprise."

"That's a great idea, Benny," said Jessie.

"Well, I need to go home for lunch," said Beth.

"Will you come back this afternoon?" asked Violet.

"I don't think I can," said Beth. "But I'll try. This has been a lot of fun!" She got on her bicycle and rode away, waving cheerfully over her shoulder.

The Aldens washed their grandfather's car and went into lunch. "We have a surprise for you," said Benny as soon as they sat down.

"Oh, Benny, it's not a surprise if you tell him," said Henry.

"Yes, it is," Benny said. "He doesn't know what it is."

"When will I know?" asked Grandfather, his eyes twinking.

"Right after lunch," promised Benny.

After lunch, the Aldens all went outside. "Can you guess the surprise, Grandfather?" asked Benny.

"Hmm. I see soap and water and the hose.

Did you give Watch a bath?" asked Grandfather, trying to hide a smile.

"No!" said Benny. "We gave your car a
bath."

"He's teasing, Benny. You knew, didn't
you, Grandfather?" asked Violet.

"Yes," Grandfather answered. "It looks
wonderful. Is this part of your helper service?"

"Yes, but yours is a surprise free gift," said
Benny.

"Thank you very much, Benny. Thank
you all. I like surprises, especially surprises
like this," said Grandfather.

Just then, another surprise happened. A
familiar white truck pulled up in front of the
house.

"Another customer, it looks like," said
Grandfather. "Keep up the good work!"
He went back in the house, and Jessie,
Henry, Violet, and Benny went toward the
truck.

"It's him," said Jessie. "Charlie."

Henry walked up to Charlie's window.

"Hello," he said to Charlie. "Would you like for us to wash your truck?"

"I sure would," said Charlie. He held out a dollar. "My truck could use a good cleaning."

Watching Charlie closely, Henry said, "All the money we make is going to support building a new wing on the Greenfield Hospital. We've got a helper service."

Jessie nodded. "Did you see our signs in town?"

"I know that," answered Charlie. "I saw you at the Millers. In fact, I used to work for Mr. Miller. But I've been too busy lately with other jobs. When I saw your signs I recommended that he call you."

"You did?" asked Benny.

"Sure did," Charlie told Benny. Charlie grinned. "Why not? Plenty of work for everyone. And that's how I got started in my business, doing the same things you are doing. You're smart kids."

"Oh," said Jessie. "Well."

The Aldens all looked at each other. Dr.

Jackson wasn't the one trying to destroy their work, and Charlie didn't seem to be either.

Not knowing what else to say, they got to work washing Charlie's truck.

Several more cars came, and the children worked all afternoon. Just as they were finishing, a familiar figure rode up on her bicycle.

"Beth, you came back," said Violet.

"You changed clothes!" said Benny.

"Oh." Beth looked down at her red T-shirt and white shorts. "Yes, I did."

"We've finished washing cars, but you can help us clean up," said Jessie.

"Clean up? *That* doesn't sound like fun," said Beth crossly. "Why does everyone else have all the fun?" She jumped on her bike, leaving the Aldens to stare after her with open mouths.

"That does it!" said Jessie.

"Wait," begged Violet. "At least give Beth a chance to explain."

"I think she *should* explain what's going

on," Jessie answered. "We'll call her tonight and ask her to come over tomorrow. I have a few questions I think she should answer."

"Yes," said Henry. "I think we all do."

CHAPTER 11

One Last Chance

The next morning the Aldens were out in the yard by their boxcar. Benny was throwing a stick for Watch to chase. Violet was sitting on the stump step, and Jessie and Henry were sitting just behind her, on the edge of the boxcar. No one was talking much. They were waiting for Beth.

At last they saw her walking across the backyard. She was wearing green shorts and a white shirt with matching green trim.

"Hi," she called. "What's going on?"

"Hello, Beth," said Jessie seriously.

Violet looked at Jessie, then back at Beth. She gave Beth a friendly smile. "Hi, Beth," she said. "Do you want to sit down?"

Beth looked uneasy. "Is something wrong?" she asked.

The Aldens exchanged glances. Then Jessie said, "Beth, you remember when someone took our art supplies and ruined the posters we'd left in the boxcar."

Beth nodded.

"Someone also tore down one of our posters," said Henry. "The day you said you were at the dentist." He paused, but Beth didn't say anything.

"And someone ruined the Millers' garden so we had to do it over," Violet pointed out.

And don't forget when we couldn't find the key to get into Ms. Singh's house to feed the cats," said Jessie.

Beth still didn't say anything.

Jessie took a deep breath. "At first we thought someone didn't want us to help the hospital. We thought maybe it was Dr. Jackson, because she was against the new wing being built and thought that a new hospital should be constructed in Silver City."

Violet said, "But now we don't think it is Dr. Jackson. You and I went to baby-sit for her, remember? And she doesn't seem like the one who would be doing all these things."

Beth frowned.

Jessie went on, "For a while we thought it could be Charlie the Fix-it Man. We thought we might be taking business he might have gotten. But then Charlie came to our car wash. And he told us he recommended us for some jobs. So it doesn't seem like he could be the one."

Violet said softly, "Sometimes, Beth, you don't seem like the same person. For instance, that day you were supposed to be at the dentist, we saw you on your bicycle in town. We called you and you wouldn't stop or answer us," said Violet.

Everyone waited. But just as Beth seemed about to say something, Benny shouted, "Look, look!"

Another Beth was coming across the back-yard!

This Beth was wearing blue shorts and a blue striped shirt. She stopped in front of the first Beth and put her hands on her hips.

Benny looked from one to the other with his mouth open. Watch began to bark excitedly.

"Beth?" said Violet uncertainly, looking from one to the other.

But neither Beth seemed to have heard her. They glared at each other. Then the second Beth said, "You're doing it again!"

"Well, so are you!" cried the first Beth. "How did you know I was here, anyway?"

"I guessed that phone call last night was for me," said the second Beth. "I followed you this morning. And I was right!"

"You followed me?" said the first Beth.

"Why not? You've been following *me* all week," said the second Beth.

The Aldens stared in amazement. There were two Beths. And they looked exactly alike.

"What is going on?" demanded Jessie.

But she still didn't get an answer. Instead the first Beth burst into tears. "I just w-wanted to have some friends. Like you, Beth," she cried.

"Oh, don't cry. Don't cry," said Violet, jumping up. "It's okay . . . Beth?"

"I'm not Beth," sobbed the first Beth. "I'm Heather!"

"You're twins," said Jessie suddenly.

Beth nodded. "Yes. Heather and I are twins." She didn't look happy about it.

"Do you take turns being each other?" asked Benny.

"No!" said Beth. "*She* has been following me around ever since we moved to Greenfield. Pretending she's me. And causing trouble."

"I know what I did was wrong. I guess I was just jealous," said Heather, who had stopped crying. She rubbed the tears off her cheek on the sleeve of her shirt. "You always have friends. Every time we move you meet new people. I never do."

"Well that's not my fault, is it?" asked Beth. She turned to face the Aldens.

They listened in amazement as Beth told them how, every time they moved, Heather grew jealous of Beth's new friends and tried to ruin their fun, sometimes even pretending to be Beth. It had been Heather, not Beth, who was responsible for all the nasty tricks over the past week.

"You mean you took our art supplies and ruined Benny's bicycle tires?" gasped Violet.

Heather nodded shamefacedly.

"And ruined our posters and our garden?" asked Henry.

"Yes," said Heather softly.

"I wasn't sure at first," said Beth. "Then I saw Heather in town when we went to get new art supplies. I went after her. But she was too quick for me, and she disappeared. And, of course, by the time we got back outside, she'd let the air out of Benny's tires."

"That's why you were so jumpy," said Jessie. "And those times you acted so strange — like in the ice cream parlor that night."

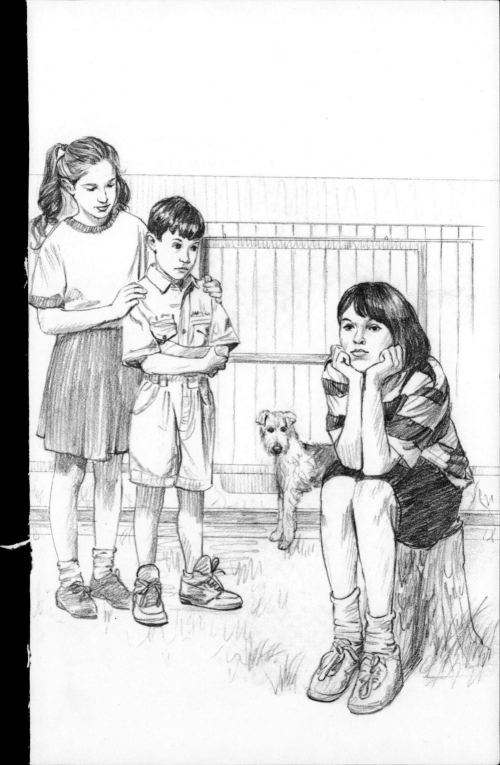

"That wasn't me, that was Heather," explained Beth. "That's how she found out about all of you in the first place."

"And that day we saw you in town, when you said you had to go to the dentist?" asked Violet.

Beth looked startled. "I *did* go to the dentist."

"You're right. That was me," said Heather. "And that was me, baby-sitting, too. I got the phone call and pretended to be Beth."

"But Beth," said Jessie. "Why didn't you just tell us you had a twin?"

"Because she always ruins everything. I can't trust her!" cried Beth.

Violet looked at Heather. "Heather? You've done some really mean things. Why couldn't you just be friendly, like Beth?"

Heather looked ashamed. "I was afraid you wouldn't like me. Everyone always likes Beth, not me."

"Maybe that's because you don't give people a chance," Henry said.

Beth was looking at her twin sister. "I never understood why you did all those mean things before. I guess I never realized how you felt, Heather," she said.

"I'm sure you all must hate me for what I did," Heather said. "But I promise I'll never do anything like that again. Will you give me another chance?"

Just then Mrs. McGregor opened the back door of the house. "Phone call for the helper service," she called.

"Come on," said Jessie.

"What about me?" asked Beth. "Do you still want me to come along?"

"Of course we do," said Violet. She looked from Beth to Heather. "Let's *all* go help out."

"Even me?" Heather asked.

"Yes, you, too," Jessie said. "If you want to."

"I *would* like to," said Heather.

"Then let's go!" said Benny.

"A twin can make twice as much trouble," Benny said. "But you know what? Maybe having a twin can be twice as much fun, too."

GERTRUDE CHANDLER WARNER discovered when she was teaching that many readers who like an exciting story could find no books that were both easy and fun to read. She decided to try to meet this need, and her first book, *The Boxcar Children*, quickly proved she had succeeded.

Miss Warner drew on her own experiences to write each mystery. As a child she spent hours watching trains go by on the tracks opposite her family home. She often dreamed about what it would be like to set up housekeeping in a caboose or freight car — the situation the Alden children find themselves in.

When Miss Warner received requests for more adventures involving Henry, Jessie, Violet, and Benny Alden, she began additional stories. In each, she chose a special setting and introduced unusual or eccentric characters who liked the unpredictable.

While the mystery element is central to each of Miss Warner's books, she never thought of them as strictly juvenile mysteries. She liked to stress the Aldens' independence and resourcefulness and their solid New England devotion to using up and making do. The Aldens go about most of their adventures with as little adult supervision as possible — something else that delights young readers.

Miss Warner lived in Putnam, Connecticut, until her death in 1979. During her lifetime, she received hundreds of letters from boys and girls telling her how much they liked her books.